Martin Baltscheit has written and illustrated over forty books for children. He has won both the German Youth Literature Award and the German Youth Theatre Prize. This is his English-language debut. Martin lives in Dusseldorf, Germany. Visit Martin's website at baltscheit.de.

Marc Boutavant is a graphic artist, illustrator, and comic strip creator. His books include *Dumpster Dog* (Enchanted Lion), *Ghosts* (Enchanted Lion), and *Around the World with Mouk* (Chronicle). The Mouk stories were adapted into an animated TV series in France. Marc lives in Paris, France.

First published in the United States in 2020
by Eerdmans Books for Young Readers,
an imprint of Wm. B. Eerdmans Publishing Co.
Grand Rapids, Michigan

www.eerdmans.com/youngreaders

Original title of the Work: *Votez pour moi!*
© 2012 Éditions Glénat
Text by Martin Baltscheit:
originally published in the German language
under the title *Ich bin für mich- Der Wahlkampf der Tiere*,
©Beltz GmbH & Co KG, Weinheim, Germany

English language translation © Eerdmans Books for Young Readers

Manufactured in China

29 28 27 26 25 24 23 22 21 20   1 2 3 4 5 6 7 8 9

Library of Congress Cataloging-in-Publication Data

Names: Baltscheit, Martin, 1965- author. | Boutavant, Marc, illustrator.
Title: Vote for me! / Martin Baltscheit ; Marc Boutavant.
Other titles: Votez pour moi! English
Description: Grand Rapids : Eerdmans Books for Young Readers, 2020. |
  Audience: Ages 4-8. | Summary: "The lion always wins the animals'
  presidential election. But when a little mouse starts campaigning, the
  other creatures realize they, too, have something to say"—Provided by
  publisher.
Identifiers: LCCN 2019030894 | ISBN 9780802855435 (hardcover)
Subjects: CYAC: Politics, Practical—Fiction. | Animals—Fiction.
Classification: LCC PZ7.1.B362 Vot 2020 | DDC [E]—dc23
LC record available at https://lccn.loc.gov/2019030894

MIX
Paper from
responsible sources
FSC® C144853
www.fsc.org

Martin
Baltscheit

Marc
Boutavant

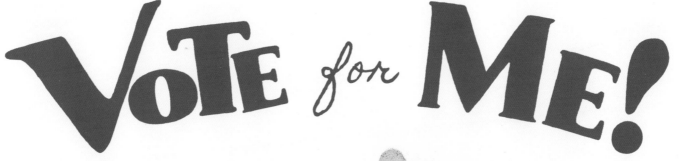

Eerdmans Books for Young Readers

Grand Rapids, Michigan

Every five years, the animals elected a president.
The lion loved elections, because the animals always voted for him.

He would stand on top of the hill and ask, "Who's voting for me?" With one voice, all the animals would reply, "We're voting for you!" And then they would all have as much cake and strawberry-coconut juice as they wanted.

But one day, the little gray mouse asked, "What's the point of elections if we can't choose between several candidates? You need some competition, otherwise it doesn't make sense!"

The lion took up the challenge and had a poster made with his portrait. He was very proud because the picture the lioness painted looked very much like him.

But the little mouse also asked an artist to make a poster for her.

When the animals saw the mouse's poster, they all wanted to make speeches and participate in the elections too.

Each animal sent a representative to the assembly to elect the new president.
Every candidate had time to speak.

The little gray mouse, who represented the rodents, made a moving speech.
"Cats should not have the right to eat mice!" she exclaimed—and all the mice applauded.

"If I become president, we will eat cats!"

Just after her, a very distinguished cat spoke: "If I become president, mice will be our staple food. We'll have them for breakfast, lunch, and dinner—grilled mice, roasted mice, mouse soup . . ."

"Vote for me and you will always have fresh mice to eat!"
All the cats clapped their paws enthusiastically.

Next, an ant spoke up: "You all need to work more! Twenty hours a day is not enough!" She raised her arms in the air in a sign of victory.

In the silence after this extraordinary declaration, one of the sheep exclaimed: "My wool belongs to me! If I become president, there will be no more shearing and knitting!"

The carp had some great ideas for a retention pond to ensure that all the animals would have water in case of a drought.

But nobody could understand her gurgles, and everyone thought she was just spouting nonsense.

The ostrich made a long speech about an airport she wanted to build, with shops, parking, four airstrips, and an underground railway line.

But when asked who would pay for all these beautiful projects,
she just buried her head in the sand.

The German shepherd spoke up in defense of law and order: he wanted
to keep everyone on a leash.

The fox pleaded for an end to all borders, all the while looking sideways at the chicken coop.

The wildebeest promised a paradise where everyone would be equal—they would eat the same things, dress the same way, sing the same songs, and live with love and fresh water.

Only the whale was not interested in these elections, and she returned quietly back home.

Once the speeches were over, it was time to vote. Since nobody wanted to show who they were voting for, they kept the ballots secret.

That evening, the mole counted up the ballots and announced the result: "Every candidate received one vote, except for the lion, since he did not vote."

The lion had lost the election! Disappointed, he decided to spend some time by himself.

The lion's former electors rejoiced. Now everyone had the president they had chosen. The newly elected officials immediately began to follow through with their promises. The fox chased the chickens, the cats munched on the mice, the mice attacked the cats,

the sheep defended their wool, the wildebeest fought for peace, the German shepherd put all the carp on leashes, and without waiting, the ostrich buried her head in the sand—where she found herself nose to nose with the mole, who had dug a long, deep tunnel to escape all the mess.

Total chaos reigned for two weeks. No one followed any laws, and all the animals did exactly what they wanted. The lion looked down from the top of the hill and shook his head. Suddenly, the little gray mouse appeared at his feet and asked:

"Well, now what are we going to do?"
The lion looked away. "What are *we* going to do?"
The mouse sighed. "Come on, old grumpy!
What would the former president do?"

The lion and the little mouse went down the hill toward the others. The former president took a deep breath and gave the biggest roar he had ever roared: "STOP! We need to start over!"

Startled, the animals froze. They looked at each other. Scratched, bitten, exhausted—
they no longer wanted to play at being presidents. And so they accepted the lion's suggestion.

Surrounded by all the chaos and unhappiness, the lion asked, "Who votes for me?"
Full of hope, the animals answered all together: "We vote for you!"

The lion had been elected unanimously again—but this time he decided to appoint the other animals as his advisors, according to their talents. And once again they all celebrated with cake and strawberry-coconut juice.